We're Little Adventurers, one and all.
Not too little. Not too tall.

My name's Peanut!
And my name's Sprat.
Me? I'm Floss with Podge my cat.
And my name's Finnegan. Snub's my teddy! 4-3-2-1, now we're ready!

We meet each week, in our shed HQ,
ready to share our fun with YOU.

A

little ADVENTURER

*** IS KIND TO ANIMALS ***

(Even ones that need a bath.)

*** HELPS OTHERS OUT ***

(of bed, trees and large holes.)

*** IS BRAVE ***

(Even when they're secretly feeling wobbly inside.)

*** IS HONEST AND TRUE ***

(Yes! Yes! Yes!)

*** DOES HIS OR HER BEST ***

(But will get help opening jars or making paper darts.)

little ADVENTURERS

SANDY SAND SANDWICHES!

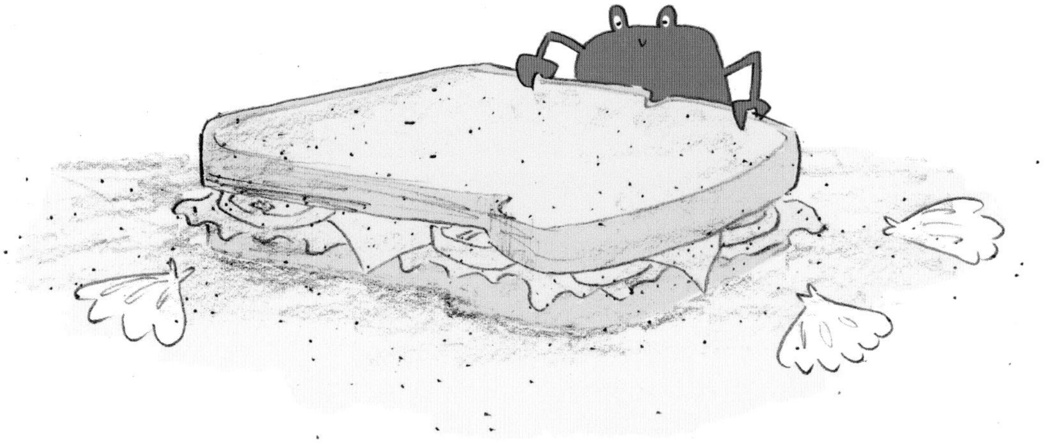

PHILIP ARDAGH
ELISSA ELWICK

WALKER BOOKS
AND SUBSIDIARIES
LONDON • BOSTON • SYDNEY • AUCKLAND

It’s time for a little adventure! Hooray!
Here are the Little Adventurers,
heading to their shed HQ.

What are they up to today?
And *where’s* Finnegan?

little
ADVENTURERS

IT'S A DAY AT THE BEACH DAY!

It's a hot, hot day and the Little Adventurers are going to the seaside. It's a chance to award each other sticky stickers!

I've brought my snorkel!

"I've got my new swimming costume!" says a proud Floss. "It is VERY fashionable and colourful."

And I've got my shrinking net!
Shrimping net!
I knew that...

But still no Finnegan.
Hmmm...

Here's Finnegan!

Look! He is already wearing his snazzy trunks.

Those trunks are sna-a-a-zzy!

"Ready?" asks Floss. **"READY!"** the others shout.

Finnegan's daddy is going to drive them to the beach in his car.

Seat belts on! Licky Dog is very happy to see Sprat, Peanut and Floss.

"Let's sing the Little Adventurers' song!" says Finnegan. His singing is *very* loud. "Let's NOT," says Peanut

"WE'RE LITTLE ADVENTURERS, ONE AND ALL! NOT TOO LITTLE, NOT TOO TALL!"

The Little Adventurers arrive at the beach. They pull on their swimming costumes, smear on some sunscreen and grab their things.

Peanut is bursting with excitement. "The sea! The sea!" she squeals.

They all run down to take a look.

The water DOES look totally
tempting, but they know
not to jump in. Not yet.

So, Sprat has an argument
with a crab!

Licky Dog licks
sunscreen!

And Floss shows a beach ball
who's boss.

"There will be lots of ways to win sticky stickers," says Floss. But, first, she reads out the safety rules.

little ADVENTURERS
RULES AT THE BEACH
* Always stay where Finnegan's daddy can see you.
And you can see him!
* Do NOT go into the sea without Finnegan's daddy.
He is VERY tall.
* It's OK to paddle in rock pools.
But make sure you don't squash any swimmy things.
* If you take an animal out of a rock pool, keep it in a bucket of seawater.
But DO NOT put sharks in with mermaids.
* Always put the animal back in the pool before going home.
And be sure to say "GOODBYE!"
* Don't drop litter.
We never doooooo!
* Have fun.
We will, will, WILL!
* Keep your hats on and wear sunscreen.
Yerch. STICKY!

"Let's get going!" says Finnegan.

IT'S SAND-SCULPTING TIME!

Each Little Adventurer must make something out of sand.

Peanut is making a mermaid. She loves that fishy tail.

Finnegan is making a speedboat.

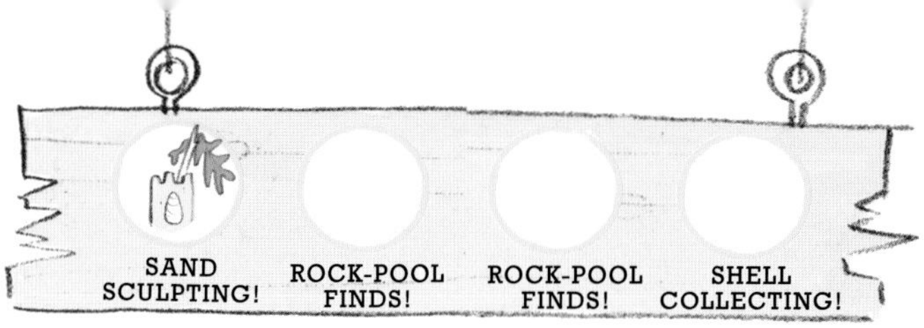
SAND SCULPTING!
ROCK-POOL FINDS!
ROCK-POOL FINDS!
SHELL COLLECTING!

Floss is building the BIGGEST castle.

Sprat is making ...
is making ... er?

My throne room will go here!
Wait and see!

All done! It's time to look at each other's masterpieces.

Everyone LOVES Peanut's mermaid.

And Finnegan's speedboat is a roaring success.

They all agree that Floss's castle is fantastic.

And now for Sprat's work of art!

"It's a very GOOD sand sandwich," says Finnegan.
Licky Dog isn't so sure.

Sand-sculpting is hard work under the hot sun. What could be better than an ice-cream or lolly? Finnegan's daddy gives Finnegan the money and they queue up at the kiosk.

Floss gets a Chocolate Surprise.

Sprat gets a Smiley Face.

Peanut gets a cone.

Pocket gets a nice nibble.

And Licky Dog? She gets an ice-cream all of her own!

LICK!
LICK!
LICK!

Finnegan? He gets a Rocket Blaster. He pays for the ice-cream and puts the change in his pocket.

After their little rest, they are ready for

ROCK-POOL FINDS!

The Little Adventurers hunt in pairs.

"I've got lots of squib-ment!" says Sprat. "You do!" Peanut smiles. "And I think you mean *equipment*."

Peanut and Sprat find a great big pool to search in…

Meanwhile, Finnegan and Floss have found a VERY rocky rock-pool.

Finnegan finds a tiny fish.
Floss spots a blob of jelly.
"That's a sea anemone!" she says.

It IS a very rocky rock-pool!

Peanut has found
a tiny crab.
"Aren't you sweet,
Mr Crab?" she says.
The crab just clacks
its claws.

Sprat has found
LOTS of interesting
seaweed, amongst
other things.

Look! A fish!
I think it's your flip flop, Sprat.

Now it’s time for **SHELL COLLECTING!**

The only rule? Not to collect shells with creatures still living inside them.

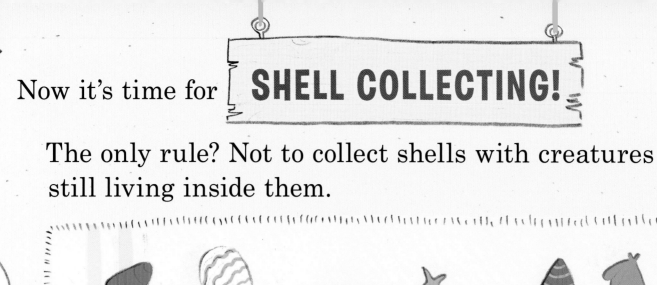

That glinty one's not a shell!
GLINT! GLINT!

SAND SCULPTING!
ROCK-POOL FINDS!
ROCK-POOL FINDS!
SHELL COLLECTING!

There are shells everywhere.
The Little Adventurers lay them
out on a towel. They come in all shapes and sizes.

THAT ONE'S MOVING!
SCUTTLE!
SCUTTLE!

"Look!" Sprat says, all excited. "Treasure!"

Finnegan puts his hand in his pocket. It's empty and his face goes white. "Oh no!" he cries. "The change has gone!"

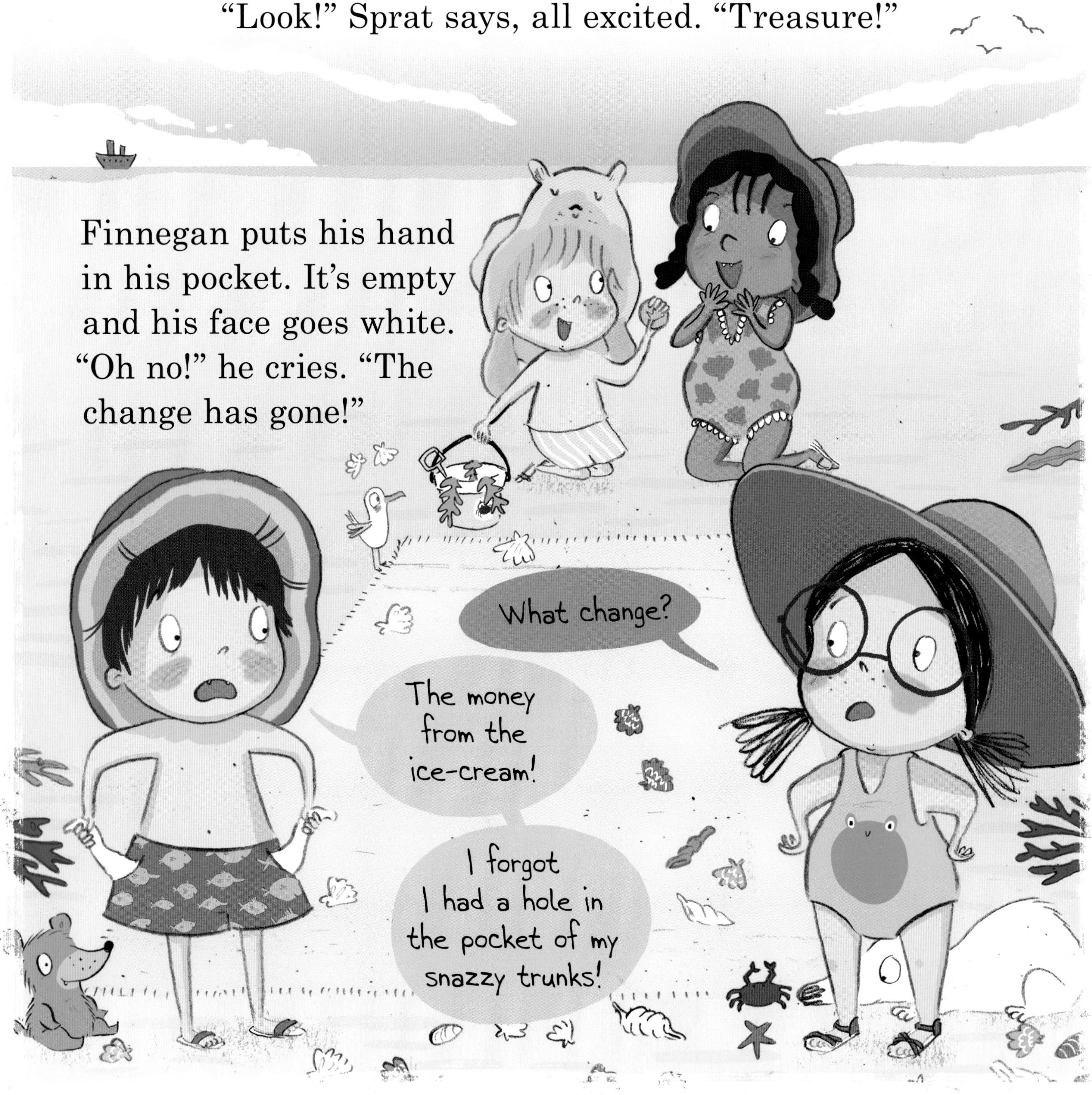

What change?
The money from the ice-cream!
I forgot I had a hole in the pocket of my snazzy trunks!

With one coin found, there are still FOUR to find! The treasure hunt is ON! (Perhaps you can help, too.)

Hooray! The coins have been found and given to Finnegan's daddy. And there's still time for a quick paddle.

On with the armbands and rubber rings then...

Splish

splash

splosh ...

into the sea!

A DAY AT THE BEACH DAY has been fantastic fun.

They've got plenty of shells to remember
it by ... AND sand in all their hats!

Back in their clothes and back at their shed HQ, it's time to give out the sticky stickers. It was *far* too wet and sandy to give them out at the beach! Even Snub gets his very-own sticker:

– FOR –
MOUSE-SITTING
POCKET
WHILE PEANUT WENT
SPLISHY-SPLASHING
IN THE SEA

I wonder what the
Little Adventurers will
get up to next time?

Don't you?

little
ADVENTURERS
SEASIDE
FACTS

SPRAT's
SEAS AND OCEANS FUN FACTS

- More than half (but less than three-quarters) of the Earth's surface is sea water.

What a soggy planet we live on!

- The deepest part of the ocean is 11km down!

Or up, if you start at the bottom.

- There are around 28,000 different kinds of fish in the sea.

That's lots and lots and LOTS of them!

- The world's longest range of mountain is in the sea. It is over 56,000km long!

But with no flags on top!

- The Dead Sea is so salty that people can't swim in it. They float to the surface!

No need for a rubber ring!

- The largest animal ever known to have existed lives in the sea. It is the blue whale. It's bigger than the BIGGEST DINOSAUR EVER!

FLOSS's
SPARKLING STARFISH FACTS

- The proper name for a starfish is sea star.

Or MISTER sea star if it is a man sea star.

- Star fish are not fish.

They are not stars either but they are SORT OF star shaped.

- There are around 2,000 different types of sea star. Most have five arms.

Or are they legs?

- They don't have a brain!

I wonder what they think about THAT?

- Sea stars have eyes at the top of each arm but they STILL can't see very well!

Imagine a sea star wearing glasses!

- If a sea star loses an arm, it grows back!

NOW, THAT IS AMAZING!!!!

FINNEGAN's SANDTASTIC SAND FACTS!

- Each teeny-tiny grain of sand is a tiny piece of rock, rubbed down by the sea over a VERY, VERY long time, or is a tiny piece of gravel or pebble or even shell.

  It must take FOREVER!

- The world's longest beach is in a country called Brazil. It is over 212 km long!

  That would be a long walk to get an ice-cream!

- In some countries, turtles lay their eggs in the sand. When the babies hatch they have to run into the sea.

  What? No pram or pushchairs? They must get VERY tired!

- The world's tallest sandcastle was JUST UNDER 12 METRES TALL.

  They must have used a BIG BUCKET to make that!

- A sandstorm is when the wind picks up sand and carries it for miles!

  You could end up with a beach in your back garden!

- Sand can be used to put out fires. You sometimes see sand in red fire buckets.

PEANUT's ALL ABOUT HERMIT CRABS

- Hermit crabs don't have their own shells. They find empty ones and move in!

  That's a clever move!

- When a hermit crab grows too big for its shell home, it moves to a new one.

  And it doesn't need a removals van!

- Sometimes, a sea anemone lives on a hermit crab's shell. That way, it gets to move around with the crab.

  Free travel!

- When the hermit crab moves to a new shell, the anemone moves too!

  Dad says ~~are~~ anemones can STING. So they can protect their crabby Shell-mate!

- Hermit crabs can live for up to 30 years.

  That's ANCIENT!!!

ARDAGH & ELWICK

Award-winning author Philip Ardagh and author/illustrator Elissa Elwick teamed up as Ardagh & Elwick to create the Little Adventurers. Although Ardagh writes the final words and Elwick draws the final pictures, they work together on making up the stories and deciding what everyone gets up to on each page, which is far too much fun. Ardagh is very tall with a big bushy beard. Elwick isn't.

To everyone who's collected interesting sea creatures in their bucket but put them back carefully afterwards. Good job!
P.A.

For Sarah McIntyre, studio mate extraordinaire
xx
E.E.

The Little Adventurers series is dedicated to the memory of Sally Goldsworthy of The Discover Children's Story Centre, Stratford, East London. She was an inspiration to so many.

First published 2019 by
Walker Books Ltd
87 Vauxhall Walk
London SE11 5HJ

10 9 8 7 6 5 4 3 2 1

Text and illustrations © 2019
Philip Ardagh and Elissa Elwick

The right of Philip Ardagh and Elissa Elwick to be identified as author and illustrator of this work has been asserted by them in accordance with the Copyright, Designs and Patents Act 1988

This book has been typeset in Century Schoolbook

Printed in China

British Library Cataloguing in Publication Data: a catalogue record for this book is available from the British Library

ISBN 978-1-4063-8562-5

www.walker.co.uk

MIX
Paper from responsible sources
FSC® C008047